AVENGERS ASSEMBLE!

© 2018 MARVEL

Meet the Avengers

United, the Avengers are Earth's best defense! Learn more about these heroes' secret identities by matching your stickers to the shadows.

Tony Stark is a billionaire inventor!

Clint Barton was once a circus performer, and a criminal!

Natasha Romanoff is a trained super-spy!

Dr. Bruce Banner is a brilliant scientist!

Super soldier Steve Rogers was once much scrawnier!

Thor is the heir to the Asgardian throne!

Heroic Puzzles

Earth's mightiest heroes are on the scene and ready for action! Complete the puzzle with your stickers.

Alleyway Rumble

Nick Fury has called his top S.H.I.E.L.D. agents to take out a group of seriously evil villains. See the fight go down with your stickers.

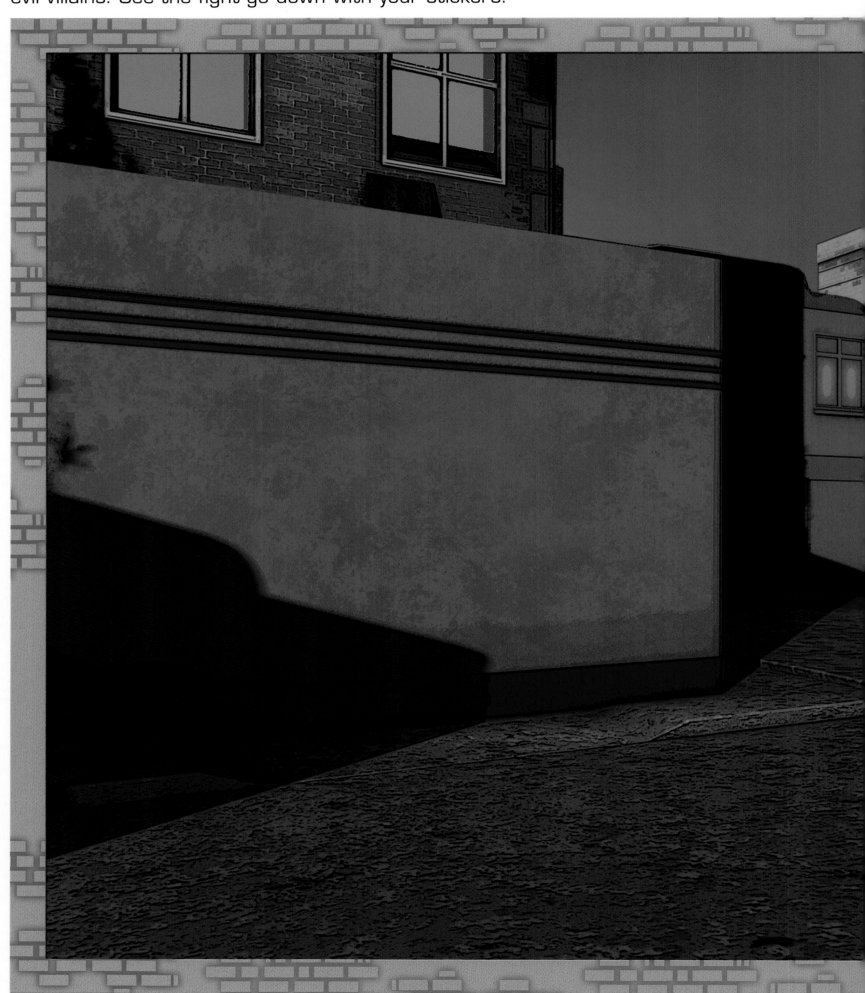

Super Snapshots

Check out the heroes below as they fly into action! Match the iconic badges to the right heroes.

Snarling Foes

Look at the villainous faces of the Avengers' arch nemeses! Fill them in with your stickers.

Zoom In On Crime

How well do you know the Avengers? Take a look at the close-ups and match the heroes to each.

Mighty Scenes

The Avengers strike a dramatic pose before they launch their next attack. Make the bottom scene match the one on top with your stickers.

SUPER VILLAIN
SHOWDOWN

Meet the Villains

The Avengers work together to take down the bad guys that no hero can fight alone! Match your stickers to the shadows to meet some of their worst foes.

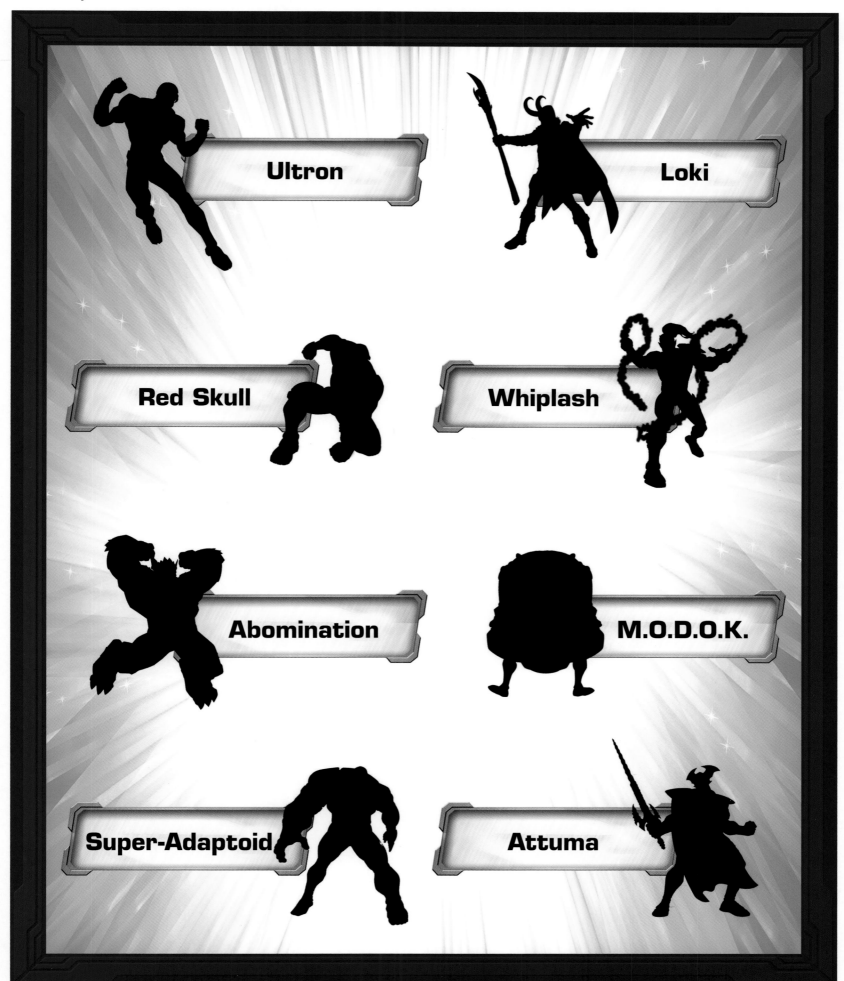

Ultron

Loki

Red Skull

Whiplash

Abomination

M.O.D.O.K.

Super-Adaptoid

Attuma

Street Attack

These super villains are launching an attack on the streets of New York! Use your stickers to help the Avengers identify their foes.

Epic Showdown

The Avengers have assembled to defend the Earth from the latest villainous invasion. Bring this fight to life with your stickers.

Know Your Enemies

S.H.I.E.L.D. keeps files on all the bad guys they face. Match your stickers to the shadows to learn more about their enemies.

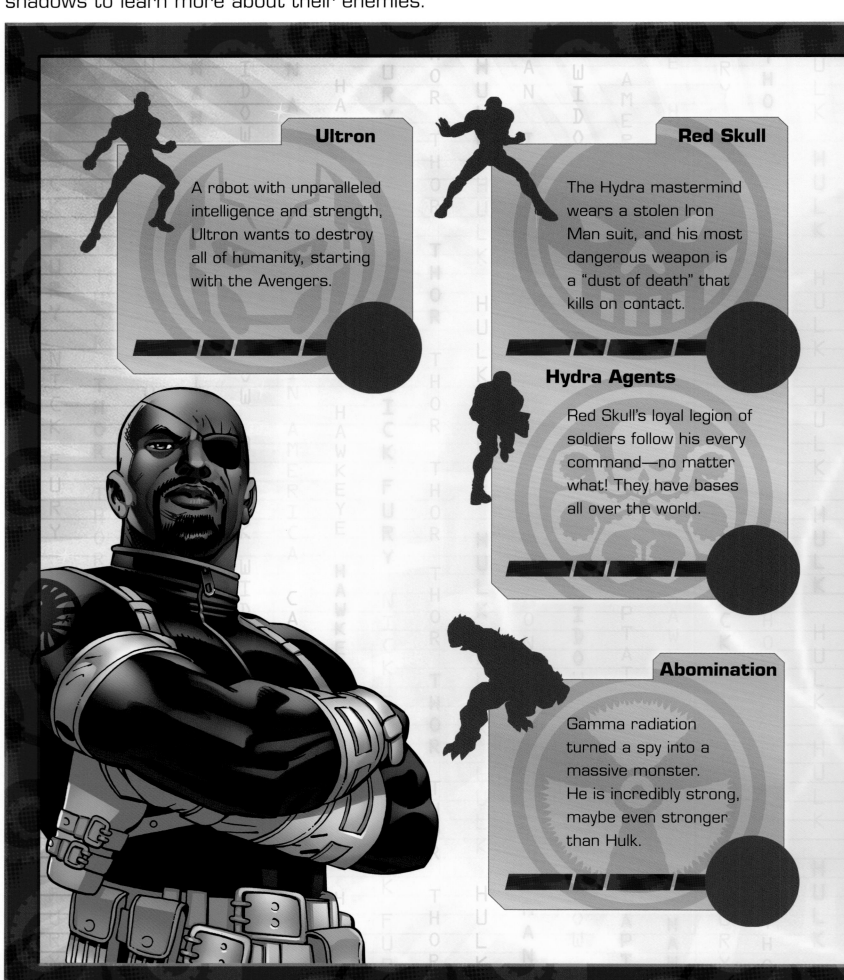

Ultron

A robot with unparalleled intelligence and strength, Ultron wants to destroy all of humanity, starting with the Avengers.

Red Skull

The Hydra mastermind wears a stolen Iron Man suit, and his most dangerous weapon is a "dust of death" that kills on contact.

Hydra Agents

Red Skull's loyal legion of soldiers follow his every command—no matter what! They have bases all over the world.

Abomination

Gamma radiation turned a spy into a massive monster. He is incredibly strong, maybe even stronger than Hulk.

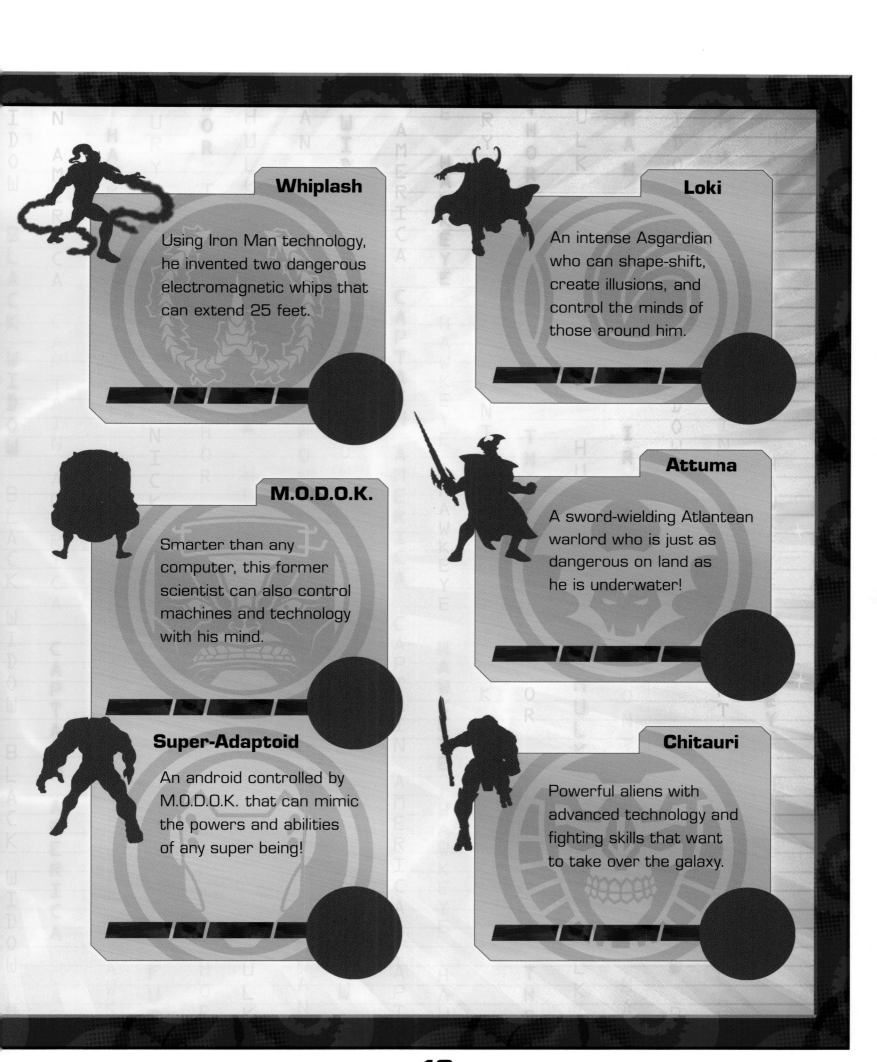

Whiplash

Using Iron Man technology, he invented two dangerous electromagnetic whips that can extend 25 feet.

Loki

An intense Asgardian who can shape-shift, create illusions, and control the minds of those around him.

M.O.D.O.K.

Smarter than any computer, this former scientist can also control machines and technology with his mind.

Attuma

A sword-wielding Atlantean warlord who is just as dangerous on land as he is underwater!

Super-Adaptoid

An android controlled by M.O.D.O.K. that can mimic the powers and abilities of any super being!

Chitauri

Powerful aliens with advanced technology and fighting skills that want to take over the galaxy.

Puzzle Action

Our heroes are facing off with this gang of dangerous super villains. Fill in the missing puzzle pieces with your stickers.

Hidden Base

The Avengers discovered a Hydra base! Help them take out Red Skull and his Hydra goons by making the bottom scene match the top one.

HEROES VS. VILLAINS

Colorful Matches

The Avengers recognize their enemies' colorful armor. Place your stickers with the pair of colors that match each villain and hero best.

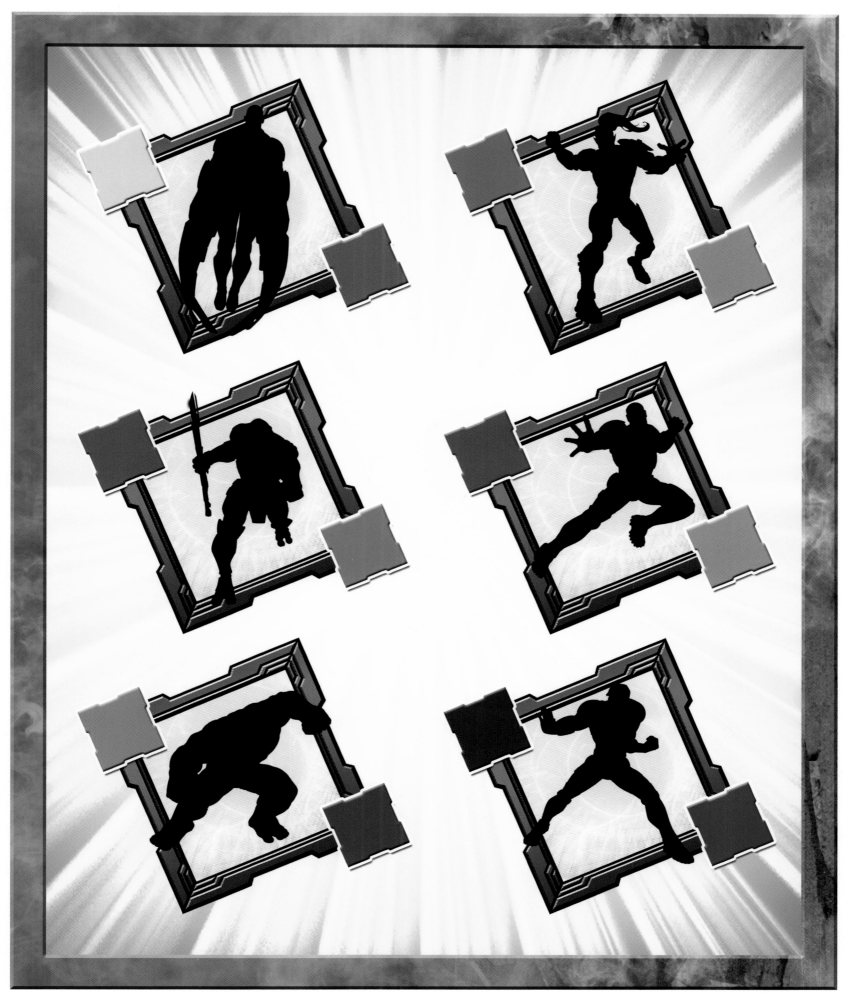

Fighting Foes

Sometimes the Avengers fight solo, and sometimes they work as a team. See who is fighting who with your stickers.

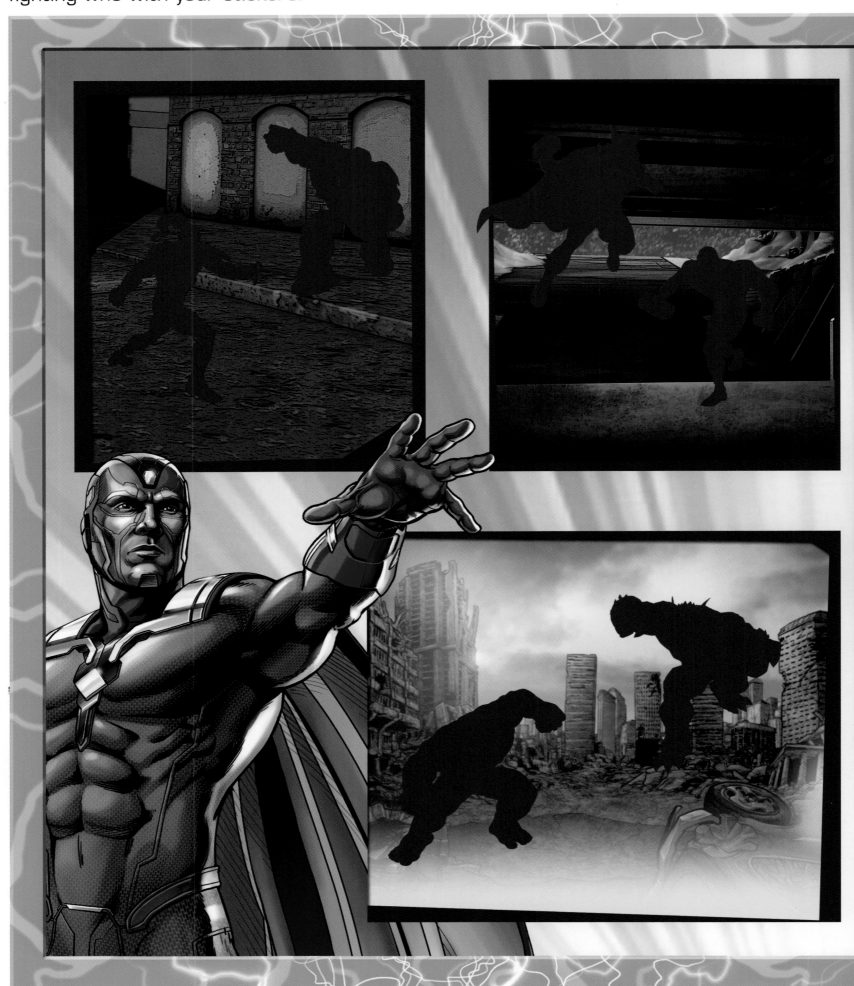

Downtown Destruction

These conniving super villains are no match for Earth's mightiest heroes! Bring the battle to life with your stickers.

Avenger Close-Up

Each member of this team has unique strengths and abilities, and together they can't be stopped! See the Avengers with your stickers.

The Hulk

Captain America

Iron Man

Black Widow

Thor

Villainous Faces

The Avengers' enemies are a fearsome bunch! Look at the faces of these scoundrels and match your stickers to the shadows.

Chitauri

Loki

Red Skull

Whiplash

Hydra Soldier

Powerful Weapons

The heroes and villains below all use powerful weapons—or they mimic them! Match each character to the weapon they wield.

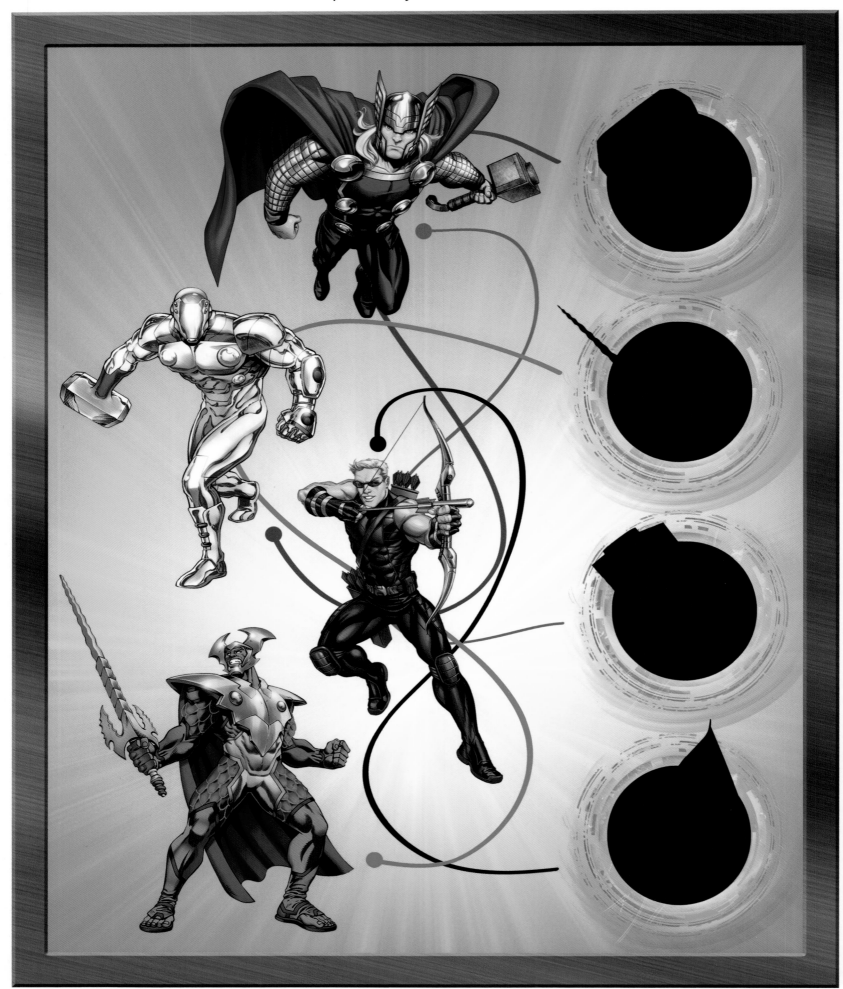

Reporting for Duty

From alleyways to mountaintops, the Avengers will track down and take down their enemies. See the scenes with your stickers.

Match the Brawls

The Avengers are keeping the city streets safe from these rampaging criminals. Make the bottom scene match the top one with your stickers.

NEW RECRUITS

Shapes & Shadows

How well do you know the Avengers? Match your stickers to the shadows to identify each Super Hero.

Vision is Artificial Intelligence come to life!

Falcon's high-tech winged harness helps him fly high!

Black Panther is king of the Wakanda!

War Machine is special liaison to Stark Industries.

Wasp has bio-electric blasters installed in her gloves!

Giant Man can grow or shrink down to ant size!

Heroic Puzzles

United against a common threat, the Avengers are always ready for action!
Complete the puzzle with your stickers.

Hanging at the Hangar!

The Helicarrier is loaded and ready for take off! Get everybody on board by placing your stickers on this scene!

Super Snapshots

Every Avenger has an iconic badge! Match the badges to the right Super Hero with your stickers!

Never forget a face!

Are you ready to face the Avengers? Place the correct sticker on each character to complete the scene.

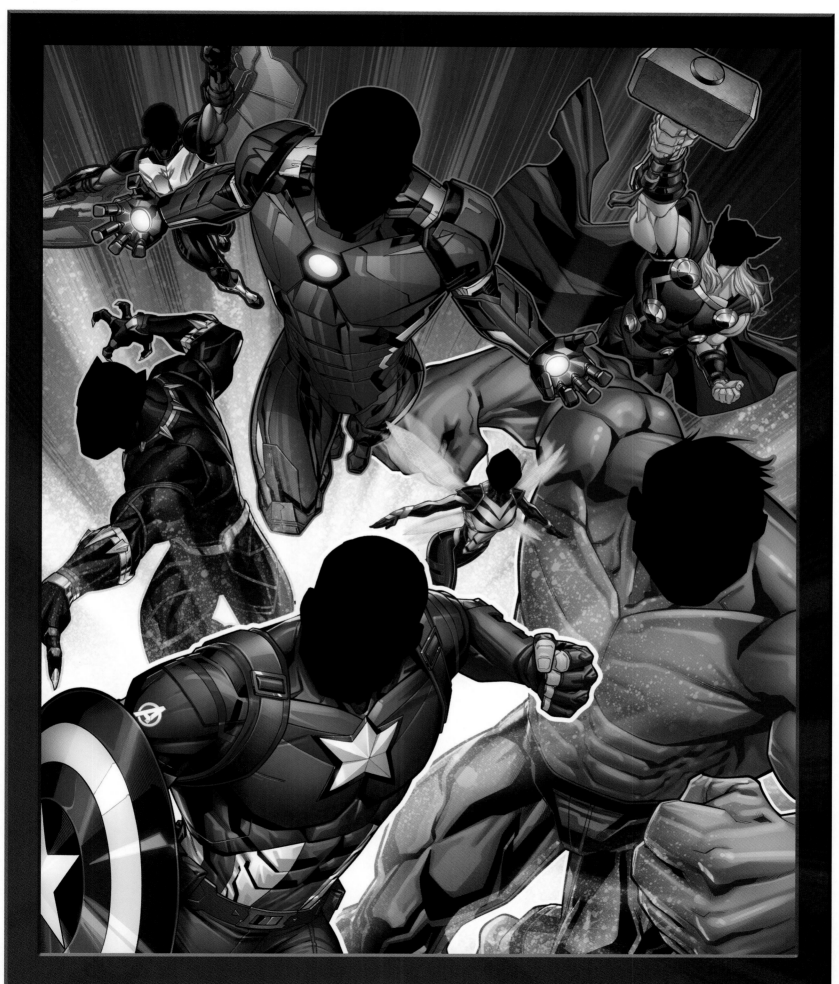

Avengers in close-up!

How well do you know the Avengers? Take a look at the close-up and match the heroes to each shadow.

Storm Warning

There's something in the air. It's the Avengers! Make the bottom scene match the one on top with your stickers.

SUPER HERO SHOWDOWN

Colorful Matches

Each Super Hero and every villain wears distinctive color combinations. Place your stickers with the pair of colors that match each villain and hero best.

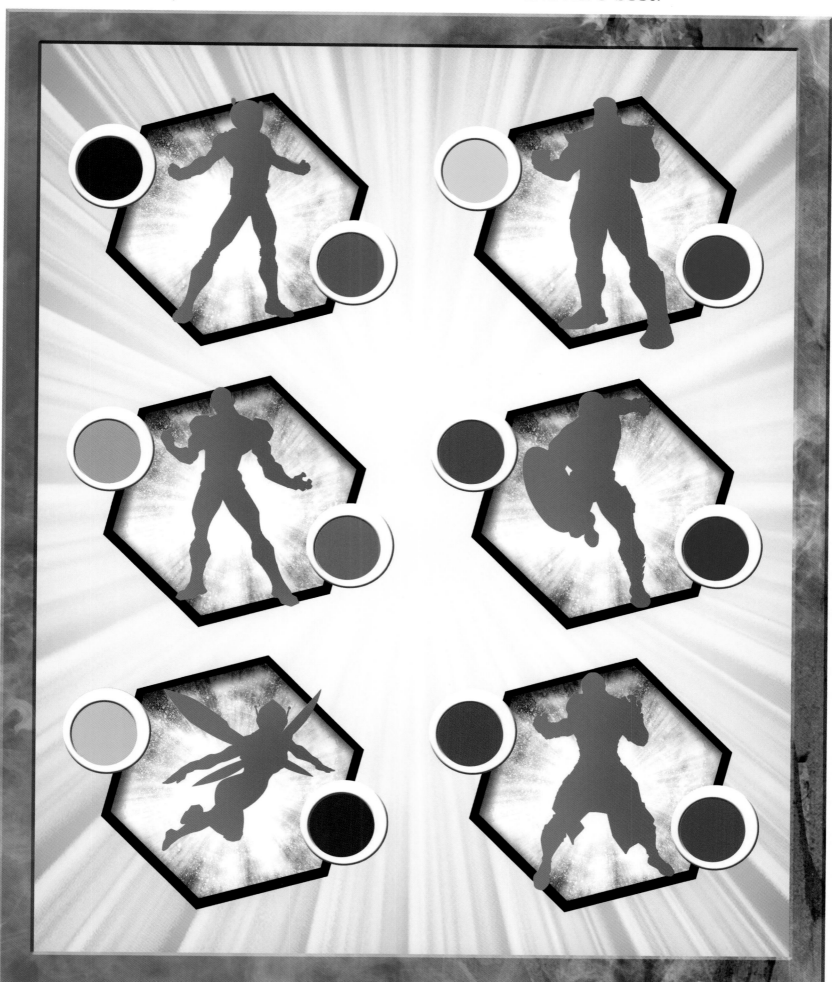

To The Rescue

No matter how near or far, the Avengers are always ready to answer a call for help. Find out who is on each rescue mission by using your stickers.

Avengers Assemble!

Earth's mightiest heroes are reporting to Tony Stark's lab for debriefing.
Bring the scene to life with your stickers.

Who's who?

Every Super Hero and each villain has special skills. Use yours to recognize them all! Match your stickers to the correct character.

Red Skull

Captain America

Wasp

Thor

Loki

Black Panther

Ultron

Vision

Thanos

Black Widow

Wielding Weapons

It takes a strong arm to wield a mighty weapon! Match your stickers to the shadows to complete each Super Hero.

Avengers Everywhere

In the sky or on the ground, the Avengers are always ready to defend the world from enemies! See the scenes with your stickers.

Ready for Action!

The Avengers are united against a common threat! Make the bottom scene match the top one with your stickers.

COSMIC THREAT

Phidal

The Infinity Gauntlet

Thanos has collected all the Infinity Gems on his Infinity Gauntlet!
Do you know what power each gem holds? Match the stickers to the description.

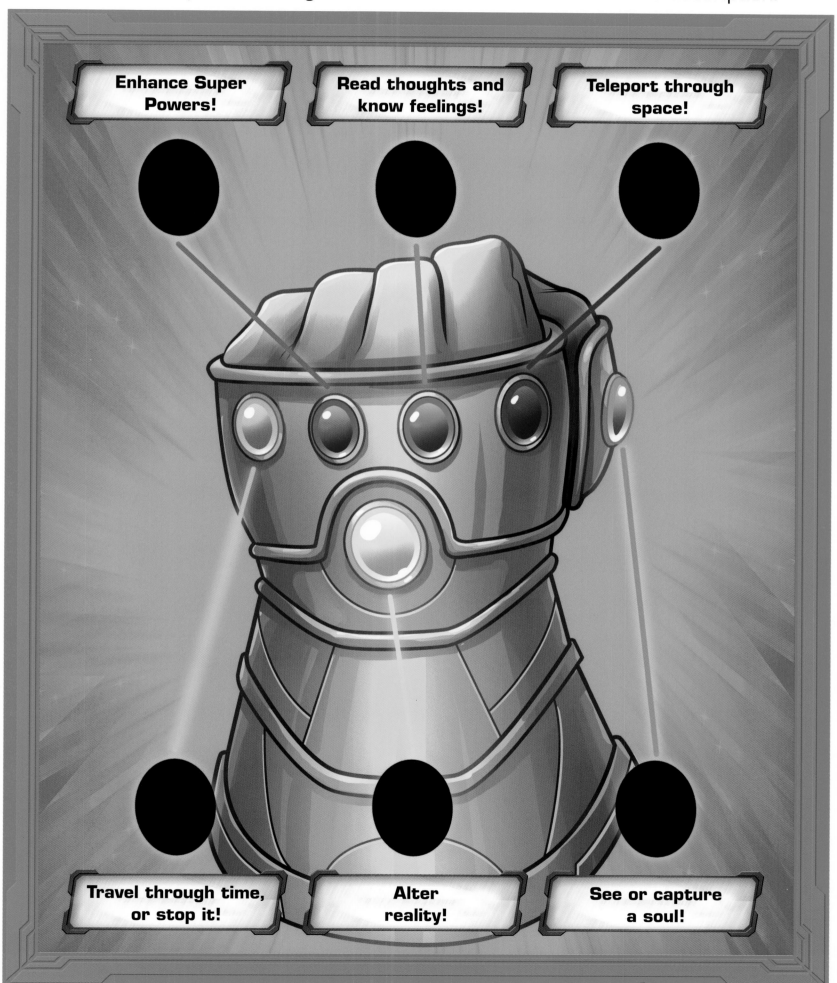

Enhance Super Powers!

Read thoughts and know feelings!

Teleport through space!

Travel through time, or stop it!

Alter reality!

See or capture a soul!

Face Your Fear!

The Avengers are gathering forces for a monumental battle! Reveal each character's face with your stickers.

Space Battle

The Avengers must stop Thanos from destroying the world! Decorate the scene below with your stickers.

Signs of Heroism

Every Super Hero has unique skills and abilities. Match your stickers to the shadows to see them all!

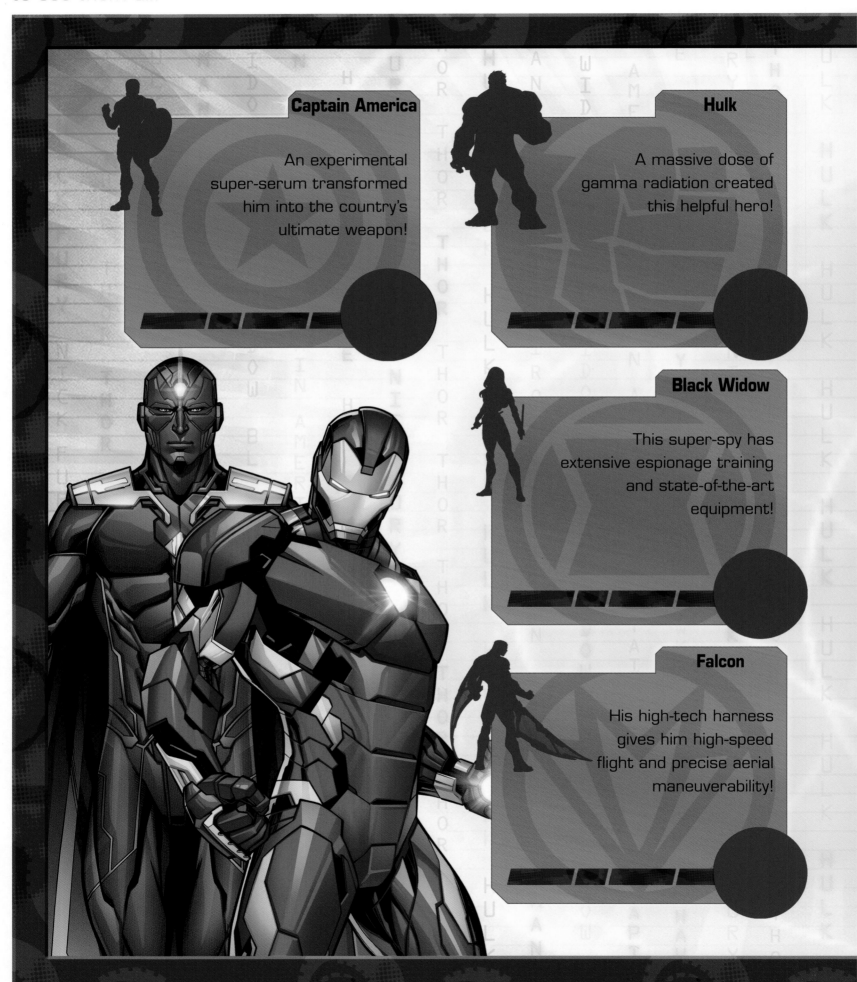

Captain America

An experimental super-serum transformed him into the country's ultimate weapon!

Hulk

A massive dose of gamma radiation created this helpful hero!

Black Widow

This super-spy has extensive espionage training and state-of-the-art equipment!

Falcon

His high-tech harness gives him high-speed flight and precise aerial maneuverability!

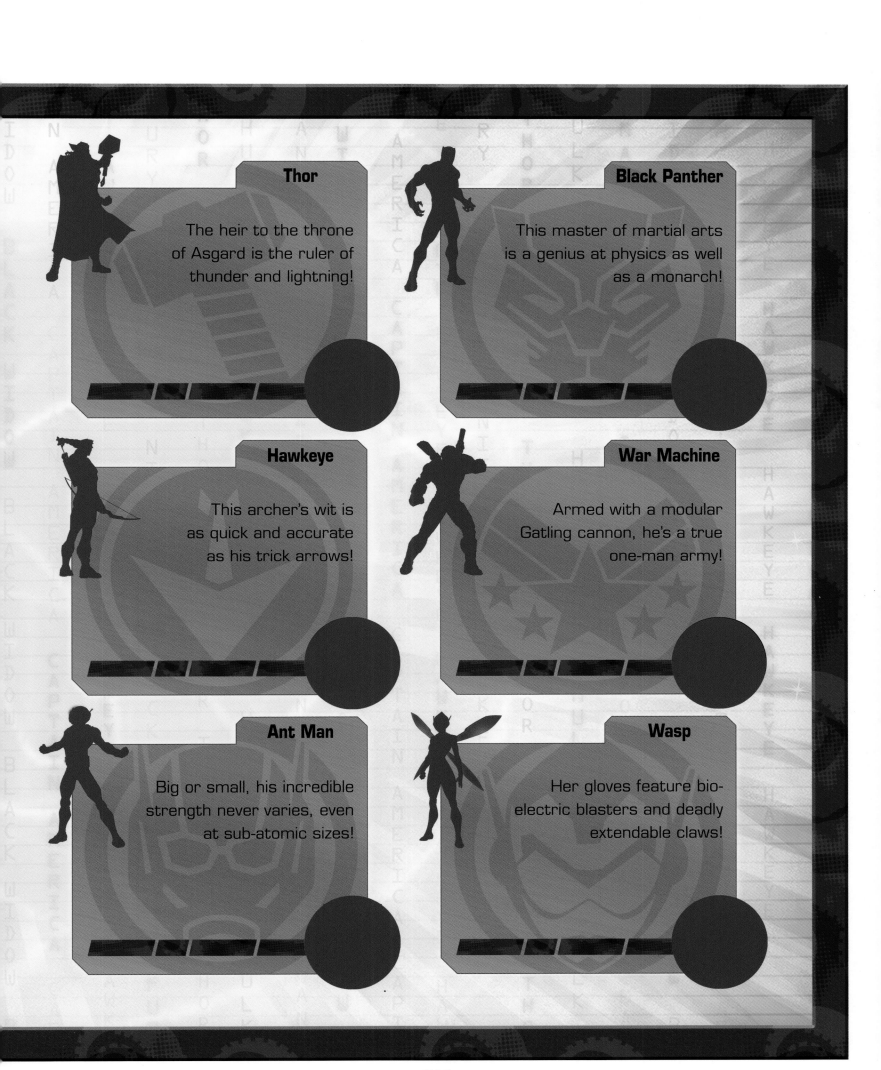

Thor

The heir to the throne of Asgard is the ruler of thunder and lightning!

Black Panther

This master of martial arts is a genius at physics as well as a monarch!

Hawkeye

This archer's wit is as quick and accurate as his trick arrows!

War Machine

Armed with a modular Gatling cannon, he's a true one-man army!

Ant Man

Big or small, his incredible strength never varies, even at sub-atomic sizes!

Wasp

Her gloves feature bio-electric blasters and deadly extendable claws!

Puzzle Action

The Avengers must battle to defeat Thanos at any cost! Fill in the missing puzzle pieces with your stickers.

It's a Match

The Avengers collaborate to ensure the fall of the mad Titan! Make the bottom scene match the top one with your stickers.